When Kids Have Grandparents As Parents

By Lauren Gould

Illustrated by Mary K. Biswas

ISBN: 1723478814
ISBN-13: 978-1723478819

For Jason

Dedicated to all the grandparents who are parents once again.

www.whenkidsseries.com

In art class every year, we draw our family picture. I love art class and I always do my best. My finished picture always looks different from my classmates' pictures.

Topic - Family Picture

Since I am just a kid no one has told me why, but I live with my Grandma and Grandpa, and not my Mommy or Daddy. It has been this way since I was a baby.

SCHOOL BUS
SCHOOL BUS

My family picture will hang on the fridge. Grandma hangs all my artwork on the fridge. I always draw it the same, just me and Grandma and Grandpa. We hold hands and stand in the front yard.

Artwork
for
Daddy
rk
for
Mommy

I still draw pictures of me with Mommy and pictures of me with Daddy. I save those pictures in my special place in my bedroom until I see them again.

Sometimes, I don't see my Mommy or Daddy for a long time and I try not to be sad. When I don't see them, I stay busy with kid stuff and spend time with Grandma and Grandpa and my other family members.

On the weekends that I do see my Mommy or Daddy, I don't always spend the night with them and we have day visits. We have lots of fun together. We ride bikes, go fishing or even canoeing on the river.

Mommy and Daddy love when I surprise them with the drawings I made for them.

My parents try their best to come watch me at my baseball or soccer games.

When they can't come to my games, I try not to be upset or angry with them since I know Grandma and Grandpa will be there, and I will see my parents again soon.

My Grandma and Grandpa are my Daddy's parents. They take great care of me, just like they took great care of my Daddy when he was a kid.

I like to play baseball just like my Daddy.
I am very good at sports.

I have friends at my school who live with their Grandparents too. Some of my friends have siblings and some of them are the only kid in the house, just like me.

Some of them have schedules and spend the night with their Mommy or Daddy. Other kids, like me, wait until their Mommy or Daddy call to visit.

I am still a normal kid even though I live with my Grandparents. My Grandma talks with me about my feelings and she is a great listener.

She always reminds me that living with your Grandparents makes you no different from other kids, even kids that live with their Mommy's and Daddy's.

When you live with your Grandma and Grandpa you can still have fun. I swim with my Grandpa all the time and I bake cookies and treats with my Grandma.

My Grandparents are fun to be with. They help me with my homework and take care of me when I am sick. They make sure I use my manners and teach me to be a good kid.

I have friends in my neighborhood that Grandma takes me to have play dates with. She makes sure that I am safe and then she comes back to pick me up later.

She always wants me to have fun and just be a happy kid.

My life may seem different to some kids, but to me it is not. Living with my Grandma and Grandpa is just normal.

I am still a happy kid. I love them very much, and they love me too.

I may not know the reasons why I live with my Grandma and Grandpa, but what I do know is that my Mommy and Daddy still love me, no matter where they are and I love them too.

I love you Dad
I love you too, Son

Made in the USA
Monee, IL
27 July 2021

74381995R00021